STEALING THE MONA LISA

CHRIS GREENHALGH

Stealing the Mona Lisa

BLOODAXE BOOKS

Copyright © Chris Greenhalgh 1994

ISBN: 1 85224 286 8

First published 1994 by
Bloodaxe Books Ltd,
P.O. Box 1SN,
Newcastle upon Tyne NE99 1SN.

Bloodaxe Books Ltd acknowledges
the financial assistance of Northern Arts.

LEGAL NOTICE

All rights reserved. No part of this book may be
reproduced, stored in a retrieval system, or
transmitted in any form, or by any means, electronic,
mechanical, photocopying, recording or otherwise,
without prior written permission from Bloodaxe Books Ltd.

Requests to publish work from this book
must be sent to Bloodaxe Books Ltd.

Chris Greenhalgh has asserted his right under
Section 77 of the Copyright, Designs and Patents Act 1988
to be identified as the author of this work.

Cover printing by J. Thomson Colour Printers Ltd, Glasgow.

Printed in Great Britain by
Cromwell Press Ltd, Broughton Gifford, Melksham, Wiltshire.

For Ruth

Acknowledgements

About half of these poems, or versions of them, have previously appeared in *Bête Noire*, and I am indebted to its editor, John Osborne, for his initial faith and subsequent encouragement. Acknowledgements and thanks are also due to the editors of the following, where many of these poems first appeared: BBC Radio 4's *Time for Verse*, BBC Radio Kent, *London Magazine*, *The Observer*, *Oxford Poetry*, *Spectrum* and *Verse*. In addition, three of the poems collected here were selected for inclusion in *Poetry with an Edge* (Bloodaxe Books, new edition, 1993).

A number of these poems comprised part of a manuscript which won an Eric Gregory Award in 1992. Versions of four of these appear in *The Gregory Anthology 1991-1993* (Sinclair-Stevenson, 1994).

An early draft of 'Moonshots' won a prize in the Skoob Books/ Index on Censorship International Poetry Competition in 1992.

My thanks also to Chris Fletcher, Marita Maddah and Andy Waldron for their help and suggestions in putting the book together.

COVER PAINTING:

Racing Thoughts by Jasper Johns, 1983 (detail: right panel). Encaustic and collage on canvas, 121.9 x 190.8 cm (frame 127.6 x 196.2 cm). Collection of Whitney Museum of American Art. Purchase, with funds from the Burroughs Wellcome Purchase Fund; Leo Castelli; the Wilfred P. and Rose J. Cohen Purchase Fund; the Julia B. Engel Purchase Fund; the Equitable Life Assurance Society of the United States Purchase Fund; The Sondra and Charles Gilman, Jr. Foundation, Inc.; S. Sidney Kahn; The Lauder Foundation, Leonard and Evelyn Lauder Fund; the Sara Roby Foundation; and the Painting and Sculpture Committee.

Contents

The movement is from right to left, like that of writing in the Semitic languages, like the motion of a mother when she instinctively shifts her baby to her left arm to hold it closer to her heart. It feels natural, this direction, and slightly uphill. We gaze at these dreamlike tapestries of travel confident that no progress will be made — we will awaken in our beds.

JOHN UPDIKE Just Looking

Mythologies

The police and other opponents one fears
should be imagined in their underpants.

WILHELM REICH

'Today there is no news,' only the past
like a film hand-coloured frame by frame,
with cracker-barrel wisdom from Heaven
on the soundtrack, stock-footage of the capital

and the latest political hot-potato
(marked with a small WARNING tag).
We have moved beyond the authentic act.
The President, routinely evasive,

amiably corrupt, leaves his golf-buggy
to practise a gawky swing;
the Pope advertises *Hitachi*
on his cassock; the P.M. wishing

people to believe he works through the night,
leaves the light on in his study,
and the mystic few who know the formula,
like Royalty, never fly together.

The bottle's slender neck, the subtle bust,
cossetted waist and flare of the hips,
that tongue-like, lip-licking flourish
curling through the loop of the 'l'.

I lift the lid on the real thing. Pshhh...

Coffee-Break

Half-expecting a tentacle to come up
from the sink's underworld of gunge
and grab me, I gingerly immerse
my hand to search for a spoon,

breaking from the work on my play – so far
there's the watery-eyed son of a lens-grinder,
a man whose handshake transmits an electric shock,
an Elvis impersonator, a census enumerator,

a funambulist, and a Humanist
ruled by the right hemisphere of her brain:
'Everyone is capable of walking a tightrope -
something in the trick of the inner-ear...'

'More people, today, are reading *King Lear*,
and as a result are having fewer children!'
and 'You must appreciate the impact
of power-cuts on demographic patterns!'

There is no plot but it hangs together
somehow like the *Bostik*, poinsettias,
demijohns and half-jar of *Vick* that
seem an established part of the sill.

The Night I Met Marliyn

Ask not what your country can do for you,
ask what you can do for your country.

J.F. KENNEDY

The night I met Marilyn it was raining,
for I remember her petulantly shaking
her hair free from a scarf,
     and that pampered animality
in response to the cold – part come-on, part disdain,
the dangerously volcanic glamour of a mouth that
lured you to the lip, and caused you to fall in.

She had us all mesmerised, resembling a stack
of televisions in an electrical store,
all receiving the same programme;
yet behind the lazy sensuality and insouciance,
the gloved white finger quizzical against the chin,
it was obvious – to me anyway – there lay
a quiet centre of hurt, an abject vulnerability.
As she looked at me, I recognised
the management behind her smile,
and she seemed to understand that I understood.

I registered in her a terrible need for love,
and what happened later that evening
I have never related.
It would have been like stealing the Mona Lisa.

I promised Marilyn that in her all-too-public life,
the privacies that we, at least, shared
would be respected.

Then that last calamitous August night:
coming home, I heard the phone
insistent behind the locked door.
By the time I had found my key
and made a grab for the receiver,
     the phone was dead.

As at the ripple-ends of an earthquake,
the shock came sometime after the event,
yet it remains a painful, intractable thought even now,
and one which I have kept secret for over thirty years.

I will say no more, other than that the oblique details
and veiled portrait of the woman I knew and understood –
feisty, ardent, marketable –
can be found in the eponymous heroine
of my latest novel, *Marilyn Runmoe*, published tomorrow:
hardback £16.99, paperback £7.99 with 20 b/w photos.

As a Matter of Fact

1

The man sitting next to me on the plane
claimed
he'd collected one sachet of sugar
from every airline in the world.

He insisted on shaking my hand and
calling me repeatedly by my first name.
He probably has many friends and lots of money
and, feeling that exaggerated sense of mortality

you get at thirty thousand feet
and with the urge, correspondingly
strong, to relate my life-story to a stranger,
I said 'no shit!' and noted parenthetically

that I had every backnumber of *Yeasty Catgirls*
ever printed, not to mention a few never
generally released. He countered with 'the fact' that
he could fold a piece of paper

in half nine times. I said I'd once eaten
a whole jar of cayenne pepper.
He rejoined that if I studied Figures 3
7, 16 and 21 in some noted medical

encyclopaedia I'd see that the model
was him. He asked me what I did for
a living and I told him I counted cars
on a raised footbridge of the Holland Tunnel,

but that I used to be a lexicographer
with special responsibility for the letter F;
that was after I'd been a synopsiser
of detective novels. He said

he'd once appeared on CNN as a quote death-
threat recipient unquote and, as I expressed my
surprise, hostesses in British Airways livery
hovered with the suavity

of café violinists, deploying contoured
plastic laptop trays
of food on every table. Outside, the sky
griddled to pink and grey.

2

The in-flight breakfast called upon my
problem-solving skills, fixing the stress-fractures
of cream-crackers together with butter and stringy jam.
Through clouds lit from above by the sun

I could see a river's energetic signature,
a bitten coastline, the ligatures of bridges,
the sea's tiny creases lit like the pores
under my glasses, the paw-prints of cloud-shadows,

and boats finessing eerily forward,
leaving wakes like pulsar patterns from the port.
The moment we crossed the water, a shifty-
looking man left his seat and made his way

with fake casualness to the front. The man next to me
was reading out the temperatures in
the different capitals of the world. The captain
addressed the passengers, saying that a man

had come to the cockpit (the iffy-looking guy)
and had an urgent message to announce. 'O MY
GOD!' My coffee-quickened heart beat at the thought.
'He's a terrorist and there's a bomb on board.'

The martinet of a cabin steward moved smartly
down the aisle, and an edgy voice came over the speakers –
timorous, with a lump-in-the-throat vibrato.
A feeling of nausea rose, then down *hysterica passio*:

'Doris, I know this is a strange time and place
to say it, but somehow it's now or never –
will you marry me...?' and everyone
first crossed themselves, then applauded.

Doris, embarrassed but happy, stood up and said 'I will!'
Her fiancé, looking less sinister, came back and they kissed.
A smile sat on my lips with the surface tension
that keeps a glob of medicine on a plastic spoon.

The man sitting next to me said he'd once misheard
l'amour for *le mort* in a play by Samuel Beckett.
I reached for a sick-bag and voided myself
for one mouthgargingly-full minute.

The Big No-No

The erotic tension is almost palpable
as they stand jiggling brandy loin-high

in warm circles: the corpulent older man
with the bonhomie of a department-store Santa,

his right arm draped round a young man's shoulders,
his left arm circling a younger woman's waist.

His glasses, at an oblique angle to the camera,
have whited-out, while the pupils of the other two

are pink as rabbits' eyes from the flash –
and if I tell you that the older man

happens to be my boss, the girl his mistress,
the other me, and that several times

her labia have given me less trouble
than a milk-carton, then perhaps you will

understand why I'm no longer employed
and why I finger this photograph with

three parts nostalgia, one part regret.

Enterprise

I

He sat signing cheques, the dark cowl of a lamp
bent low over the table,
his daughter executing parquet slides in the lounge.
Then he came through to greet me.

He looked younger than his photographs. He said
'Son, business is the science of vested
interests – what can you do for me?' I said
I knew that Rome wasn't built in a day...

and he said he didn't like to stay
in one place too long – never did – and it
took time to find a good dentist.
I said I tended to see the world through cut-glass,

apprehending things in split-second prisms. He said
that often a shard of glass embedded
in the skin for years can suddenly come to the surface.
Then his eyes quickened to a corporate spangle –

the rhythm of opaque office-windows.
He lifted his brandy glass to the light
in an attitude of fey connoisseurship,
his fingers athwart the stem, twisting it

in half-inches, examining it like a jewel.

II

A hundred years ago he would have been sweeping chimneys.
Now he owns a restaurant in Paris, real-estate in L.A.,
a flourishing sales company in Italy
and is fluent in six currencies.
'Every day is a battle,' he explains,
sweating efficiently as he brandishes
an imaginary nine-iron against the bay-window.
'You have to think positive...be a winner!' he continues.

Outside, two large car-headlamps moon
against the iron gates of the drive.
He opens the window to a smell of rain.
In the distance I hear the sea against shingle –
time enough for one wave's brief tumescence
to collapse upon the shore before the window is shut
and he's turning to me, muttering, avuncular –
'There are too many middle-men, Tony, too many middle-men.'

III

The way he parked the car was pure anal retentive,
though later in the restaurant he loosened up,
dispensing apothegms like a Christmas cracker:
'A diamond is just coal gone wrong,' or

'Playing with matches as a child
taught me nothing about fire,
but everything about numbers,
from where it was a short leap for

a bright spark to a light-sensitive calculator,
the bank's revolving door
flaunting its four-leaf clover
and a wife with an allergy to anything but gold...'

His wife dug a fork into her hand while smiling
over the dinnertable. I equitably
topped up the glasses as he continued,
his memory enjoying a renewable integrity,

his voice taking on the disembodied,
speak-your-weight voice of God:
'So you want to know the secret of my success?'
He smacked his lips and whispered:

'An easy-to-remember telephone number,
and *instinct!*'
            We clinked warm finger-printed glasses.
'Instinct!' he enjoined again.
'Instinct!' I thought to myself, but said nothing.

IV

'You must be prepared to be unpopular
if you want to be a good boss,' he said,
and with a drunken 'Shush!'
he tip-toed out of the car.

His wife drove me home,
the variable chances of lamplight and leaves
chequering her legs,

her throat hot beneath the chill of her necklace,
the splintery Xs of carlights
bursting like kisses through the glass.

The beautiful emptiness of the night
rippled under the needly glare of the headlights
yielding deceitful perspectives.

As we reached my house, darkness
puddled around the car,
the moths danced madly with desire.

An intoxicating odour of honeysuckle and narcissus
charged the wet smell
of earth and invisible greenness,

and in the warm darkness
the moon swelled
between blanched and tattered clouds...

Then, as I inched out of the car and thanked her
she drove off, leaving me
wreathed in the blue plumes of the exhaust.

I flattened the gravel in the drive with my foot,
thinking to myself:
'I will never make a good boss!'

Pentimento

During the course of dinner,
between mouthfuls of stuffed barbel,
you alluded to some new paintings,
their canvases not yet dry.
Evidently, your new mistress
(thirty years your junior
but already well-schooled,
jumping through the hoops
of your reproofs)
has revivified your interests.
Still digesting the last
of the (excellent) food, you
led us through to the studio
where with an underlit
jouissance of recognition
I saw the selfsame woman
glistening as if in
a fine sweat on the easel,
her face relaxing from
a rictus of fulfilment, her
hands, palm outward, crossed
on her head, fingers shorthand
for a tropism that involved
her whole body, and her breasts
like newly discovered stars
generating heat and light.

'Tell me,' you said, 'apart
from the breasts, what is your
opinion?'
      'I think, Telemarque,'
I began, 'I like the blue tint
in the hair, the golden freckle
on the iris, the grey warming to
yellow reminds me of Bonnard,'
I bluffed but had to smile
before something engaged my eye
'only to the side, what's that smudge,
indistinguishable in the mirror,

that blurry *mise en abyme?*' After
an hysterically pregnant pause
that seemed to open like
a wound in time, you extemporised:
'...That was a reflection of the bed
with a pattern of body-shapes
still etched on the sheets...
a question of balance, theme...'
Then you made to hurry us out,
but as you switched off the light,
didn't I glimpse a preliminary
sketch over by the window
with you, Telemarque,
just discernible in the mirror –
prone on the bed, flattened
like an electrocuted carp?

Sweetness and Light

(A Poem-Film for Federico Fellini)

Lunch on a wobbly table at a café in the piazza,
where the wine-racks are deployed like broadside cannon,
the pigeons lick at spilt ice-cream,
and flowers are ruffed at the neck like the Vatican's *castrati* –
religiose, opening slowly.
The waiter brings us regular refills of coffee,
tucking the receipts underneath a saucer.
We write our names with sugar in the froth, then
driving from the city with the sun-roof open,
half an hour and we're in the countryside:
the roads with a Roman straightness,
ploughland starred with silos of grain,
cypresses incendiary in a total theatre of sunlight,
hills stretching away like the dry ridges of my palate,
and power-pylons, a first attempt at
joined-up writing, ruled into the distance.

A rush of hot air burns like mustard up my nostrils.
My arms through the windscreen are done to a turn.
The only words she understands in English are
'businessman', 'ticklish' and 'air-conditioning',
though she knows the words of songs off by heart
as they are churned out by the radio.
A fan clicks adeptly from side to side
on the dashboard, subtly disturbing her hair,
drying her lipsticked mouth to the red O of the *Mobil* sign,
and pretty soon she's fumbling in my shorts,
knocking the rear-view mirror with her head,
and I'm trying to drive with a singleness of purpose,
keeping the car straight on the road.
Her mouth quickly finds my centre
and the simple physics of her intentions are
difficult to withstand. I pull over
onto a side-road fringed with chickenwire.
There's a dog barking, a red car newly washed
dripping in the sun, and she motions me to stand up
so I stand up through the sun-roof and
involuntarily I put my hands on my head.

I can feel the sun wrinkling the back of my neck,
see the mauve profiles of the hills, hear the dog barking
and the radio playing *HELP!* by The Beatles and
her urgent mercurial mouth and hands are coaxing me to a climax
and godknowswhy but I think of Marie Antoinette
and at the moment of release scream LET THEM EAT CAKE!

Gulf

(after Louis Aragon)

Incised with newly minted words,
having only one long and supple arm,
a luminous faceless head, and a belly
in the form of a numbered wheel,
the petrol pumps take on sometimes the air
of Egyptian divinities,
or the gods of cannibal peoples
whose idol is war.

O *Texaco, BP, Esso, Shell* –
great inscriptions of human potential!
Soon we will worship at your altars,
and the youngest among us will
perish for having lusted after
the nymphs in your naphtha.

La Bocca

My mouth can never be healed –
that snag in the line of the upper-lip
where some mute god
once pressed a finger-tip.

Increasingly, my lips take on a life of their own.
Their crinkly imprint pinkens every mirror.
Their grin extends from ear to ear.
They swell like an obese rose.

My lipstick's fierce semiotic
bleeds into Kleenex, spores over cups.
My kisses are lethal. Vampiric.
It becomes impossible to shut me up.

My mouth is a landscape of desire.
Candid. Unanswerable.
My lips are all dark matter.
Nothing escapes their gravitational pull.

They spread themselves across the sky
and smoulder into the sunset.
Men are afraid of their treacherous reds,
their convexities and soft hollownesses.

My lips are inviolable. They ripen.
My tongue is sweet and embayed.
There will be those who try
to cut out my mouth, to melt it down.

I have news for them. It will bite them.

Lachryma Christi '91

Driving South against the sun
towards the Mediterranean,
we happen upon vineyards,
a hang of stars
which burn and shine
hard and clear –
candida sidera,
each ganglia of grapes
espaliered like Christ,
strung out on the vine
in powdery blue
and violet clusters.

They contain the light
of the world
beneath translucent dust
and nurse their own fecundity.
They flare like a conflagration
and diffuse like a blush –
their crushed plenitude
assumed into juice
which thickens and spills
so that the road
is running with wine,
and we are drunk.

Later, on the hotel balcony
we inhale their radiance
and gorge ourselves
on mouthful after mouthful
of a rich sweet vintage
as it glugs and chortles
from bottle to glass
and fumes inside our throats.
We see the grapes' mute blue flames
as a luminous presence
in the humid darkness,
a purply opalescence in the night...

Nocturnal moths orbit
an outside light.
A mosquito buzzes like a shaver
in a dodgy socket.
Our timorous palates
feast on the wine
until, in the morning,
both our heads hurt.
Weeks afterwards,
nothing I do will remove
the red stain
from my white shirt.

A Song for Europe

...he that travails weary, and late towards a great city, is glad when he comes to a place of execution, becaus he knows that is neer the town.
JOHN DONNE: Sermons II

The hotel's complimentary can of rapidshave
said GOOD MORNING in four languages,
but no one could change a large note
before 9 am
the Spring morning in Paris after
it was decided there were
too many pigeons in the city.

I had caught an early flight
that Friday,
flying above clouds which looked like
explosions slowed a thousand times,
lancing through tongue upon tongue of mist
over the city,
into a white municipal silence.

The birds had become a public menace –
discharging themselves over citizens,
veering myopically
into oncoming cars.
Poison was laid in the basins overnight,
and as they preened themselves and sipped
at the early morning water

soon the boulevards were strewn
with their bodies:
urban, grey, stringy,
their glaucous throats twitching.
Couples shuffled through them
thinking Autumn had come early
or the binmen were on strike,

and in the *Champs de Mars*, the park attendants
raking them in
enjoyed the delusion of being croupiers.
A boy scraping the railings with a stick
stopped to look at the river
as it slopped and gulped and hiccoughed up
the dead birds into a soupy litter.

You could have knocked me over with a feather.
I thought of
the morning after a general election,
the boredom God felt on the seventh day,
a butcher wiping blood on his apron as an affectation.
I entered a café where a mulatto waitress
brought my English breakfast:

tomatoes, eggs and two quotation marks of bacon,
then plied me with the slow vengeful poisons
of the colonies – coffee, sugar, tobacco.
I returned to my hotel balcony.
On the TV, yellow-vested marathon runners
swarmed at the starter's gun
like bees smoked out of a hive.

Jeux Sans Frontières

Beyond the orchard's brass monkey of rotten apples,
way above the cornfields
and burned-out dock,
in the cool transparency of the evening

a parley of hot-air balloons –
scores of them –
fluoresce in the shape of a baseball shoe,
a fire-extinguisher, a wine bottle,
a Brobdingnagian Rupert Bear.

They float freakishly over the Weald;
riddling, fierce, hieratic,
clearing the wires and poplars,
buoyant in the mellowed eddies
of the late summer air.

We stop the car
to watch this birth of a new language –
the noun itself –
stalled above dog-rose, loganberries,
garden-fires, the hot reek of silage.

Spurred by each new blurt of flame
this nudging vocabulary
is its own publicity,
flying, like Lichtenstein's super-heroes,
over a succession of huge views.

We are dumb to such acts of grace,
as if our tongues, like our furniture,
were nailed to the floor.
The shadows fall like nets across our faces...

Slowly, our arms stretch in luminous eddies.
Our shoulders open, air
curdling around them like rippling petrol vapour
where pairs of wings now lift and spread.

The Man Who Called Himself Jesus

(being one half of a marvellous correspondence)

His first postcard
spoke of that
little bit of America
in us all.

The second had him
bivouacked under the stars.
The third found him
under 5 Stars.

The fourth talked of
something incredible –
fruit machines in
the middle of the desert,

a city where money
turns into light
and light into money
in an improbable symbiosis.

In the fifth he wrote of a road:
an endless recession
of telegraph poles
projected into infinity,

a simple and beatific
vibration of lines
dovetailing to
a vanishing point.

The sixth announced
he'd found God
in a quiescent desert flower
and a cactus plant.

The last I heard,
he calls himself Jesus,
has many wives, Rolls Royces,
and the Scriptures off by heart.

He always said he'd be a success.
So, when he says
the world will end in fire,
I know he means business.

Mycology

I came upon a mushroom
soaked to the gills
in a small wet paradise.

Its stem was fleshy and
attenuated, and took umbrage
under a buff-coloured dome.

At night, it grew in
the rich damp reek of earth and rain.
It was barely able to contain itself.

It assumed a shape like the memory of an event
that has not happened yet.
In the morning, its concentrated energy
held up the sky.

Arcadia

The bubble-lifts and yuccas
under the glass cupola
of the Shopping Centre
enjoy the same regulated temperatures
the year round –
a model village with its own
security guards, muzak and urinals.
Outside, the flags of all
the European nation states
float lumpily in the wind.
I exult in the flush of hot air
from the grille above the doors.
I watch myself in the monitors,
funny-angled, black and white,
with all the distorted enchantment
of seeing myself on film
for the first time.
Multiplied by pillars sheathed
in mirrored glass, I don't know
whether I'm coming or
going. Watched from all
points of the panopticon,
I stand at the top
of the escalators
in a moment of pure
operatic crisis,
ululating like Tarzan,
frantic like Fitzcarraldo
seeing the tiled paradise
of his paddlesteamer
tumble over
the Falls.

Three Athenian Moments

I

Athens has many ancient ruins
and no car-parks,
the traffic all horn
and no brakes.

In a region vulnerable
to earthquakes,
I always take the stairs,
never the elevator...

'Today is all beak and no feathers,'
Mandelstam said,
and, lying at a right-angle
to the high-risery

with no pillows to
support my head,
I know what he meant,
if not how he felt,

having lugged this bed
up four storeys,
the puddingy mattress buckling
on every landing

while the stairwell
screwed its way to the top.
The sunset has that
self-important look

like the neck of a chicken
after it has been cut,
a late splurge reddening
the blebs of hills,

setting fire to
the windows of the city.
Each time I reinvent myself,
willy-nilly,

the past keeps rising up.
My shadow falls flatly
against the wall.
I lay out the contents of my suitcase

like an haruspex.

II

The bridge over Marathon Lake
is wide enough for one vehicle only,
so when the lights fail,
two files of traffic meet in the middle.

Stubborn, unbiddable, resourceful with insults,
like opposing sides in a fledgling democracy,
the drivers switch off their engines.
At midnight they are still there.

In the distance, the trucks' fubsy, illuminated Michelinmen
rush like archangels through the dark.
The drivers get through a thousand cigarettes.
Tomorrow, Maenads will tear them apart.

III

By moonlight
the young epicene –
rolled in talcum,
got up as a putto
on a plinth –
strikes an attitude,
holds it,
then bellyflops into
the lake

Islands

The day no heavier than Spanish poetry,
all temperature and colour:
the crackle and spark of rubbed amber –
a wasp embalmed in marmalade...

'Something as mundane as the colour of a room
can affect my mood,' something not quite right
like a painting maddeningly off-ccntre
or the cicadas missing a beat,

and examining the line of masts in the harbour,
the road that curves around the island like a smile,
the wrinkle of gulls above a tilting horizon,
it's plain that what is 'not quite right'

is that you are in Ireland, and I am in Greece,
watching a cargo of fruit being winched ashore –
oranges, nectarines, hirsute peaches
blushing at their obstetric creases,

while a girl that might be you sits precariously
on one of the wharf's carious
stumps, a line of salt across her
espadrilles, a languid hand shifting the hair

that drifts across her cheek with the breeze.

Introducing 'Love'

Think of it in terms of a shape:
a bottle of perfume
a piano
a virus
or a butterfly's wing of lipstick on the side of a cup,

then watch
as with pathological capriciousness
it flits from one person to another
and with inflationary abandon
takes over the room.

Things go from black and white to colour.
Language, unable to take the strain,
comes unstuck
like an upholstery button.

The lights dim as at an electrocution.
Delicious anxieties become the engine
of self-ruin.

Regard these raggedly dark eyes,
crying,
these hands touching a photograph
like a blind man fingering the spines of his books.

from Love Songs

'I tell you, Madame, if one gave birth to a heart on a plate,
it would say "love" and twitch like the lopped leg of a frog.'
DJUNA BARNES: Nightwood

III

'Sympathetic' is the word to describe
the angle of the moon to the telegraph wires
as I stagger home totally drunk,
my eyes occluded like the stars,
and even though it's late I pick up the phone –
my only means of entry into your bedroom.
After many rings it's wonderful to
hear your voice struggling from its stages
of sleep: husky, rough-textured,
like velvet brushed the wrong way.

VII

It has happened before, this
edge-of-the-world feel:

the hum of powerlines overhead,
the marram wig on the bluff,

a flock of gulls expanding like a gas
over sunlit water,

and me, listening,
wet-behind-the-ears,

to that crackle and static
of stockinged legs

scraping excitedly
like crickets in the grass.

VIII

You blew a dandelion's atomium to bits.
I held the petals of a daisy
the way King Kong held Fay Wray –
clumsily detaching strip after strip
of her pre-scissored skirt:
'She loves me, she loves me not...'

You drew a blade of scutch-grass tautly
between finger and thumb
looking on, appalled,
as a dark bauble of blood
welled from a cut that opened up
like the perfect groove in a chess-set Bishop...

X

A subtle hello of sunlight
wrung from the shutters
notches shadows
on the wall

a red rose in a tall glass
swells at the offering

a flush concupiscence of petals
peels away,
falling to the water

wrinkled like our underclothes
that have soaked
in the bidet for hours

XI

Dark glasses. Flatulent motorbikes. Beach-mat scrolls.
Our needs are simple and few.

This café's shade affords a measured rest in
the music of the sun; the sky blue and uninflected.

We guzzle a fast-melting ice-cream
enoying the giddy hoist of a catch and

the chancy prisms in sopping nets paid out
from boat to stone.

Unseen, the sunlotion leaks into a plastic bag,
its coppery cocoa butter corrupting a paperback –

and everywhere wasps hot for its cloying prose,
saps for your sweetened Tampax.

XIII

Not for the first time,
vaguely randy, mildly dissatisfied,
we sit cross-legged
on the hotel bed

in the implacable heat,
eating plums from
a brown paper bag
serrated at the edge and damp,

until only one remains
in a glass ashtray,
bruised and purply
among drying stones,

like the brood spewed out
by Saturn, that slightly
bitter taste of your heart
in my mouth.

XIV

White terrace like a cuff peeping from a dark sleeve.
Stars bristle. Insects seethe.
Moonlight on the water like a frottage,
and your foot massage is the best since Mary Magdalene.

XVIII

We swam late, you essaying
a gentle breaststroke, me
legging it across the beach
into the sea
like a bankrupt aristo.
Now water seeps
warmly from my ear to the pillow.

XX

Later, the pent-up tensions
of a record heat-wave
crack blue nerve-ends of lightning
around the city,

leaving us rinsed
in inky shadows,
thrilled with the crisp elation
of each thunder-clap,

and, as if galvanised,
you talk in your sleep,
slipping love-notes
into the shuffle of your breathing.

In the morning, I wonder
whether to tell you
what you said
but think better of it.

A Sunlit Miracle

(after Jacques Prévert)

The morning is sticky as a linctus bottle.
Ceiling fans fillet the reasty air,
the shutters open saying 'Ah!'
At regular intervals
oranges drop with a muffled slam
from the trees onto the pavement,
describing neat parabolas into the gutter.
A man, young, surefooted, steps forward
with his back to white stucco.
He picks up one of the bruised oranges
and looks at the sky, fully
expecting to see the sun missing,
then he peels it meticulously,
discarding the rind,
spitting the pips out singly
as he walks.
He can feel the tart bite
of the juices at his throat
which quickens his sense of the morning
and the light
which seems to have no source –
just is –
as though worked by a pedal,
and for the first time in a long while
he is happy and smiling,
looking up at the sky
where he sees a flock of birds fly
with one veering impulse.
He returns home to find his wife
still asleep,
the curve of a shoulder,
the soft line of an extended arm
peeping out from the sheets,
her hair fanned out on the pillow,
her face suffused with sweet tiredness,
displaying a tenderness
that gives no hint of its daily expression.
He caresses her gently,

the little hairs between
his knuckles and finger-joints
brushing her cheek,
the metal of his ring surprising her
with its coldness, and she stirs,
opening her eyes with blissful indolence.
At the same time outside,
a priest, speccy, microcephalous,
is walking up the road with
the measured gravity of his calling.
He passes beneath the shadow
of the orange trees but, immersed in
the circling energies of contemplation,
fails to see the birds above him
(his face stuffed into a Bible)
and he fails to notice the snake
of orange peel lying on the pavement...
As the lovers examine each others' pores
the priest slips on the orange rind
and tumbles to the floor,
enduring the guffaws
of a young boy playing in the road
(the only witness to his indignity)
and as the priest throws
a reproachful glare at the boy,
the boy looks back and taunts the priest with
'Our Father Who Art In Heaven –
Stay There!'

Sin

Returning at three in the morning, we
walk through the lobby's pother of fronds,
peach-skin lamps and plum-coloured easy-chairs,
taking the stairs two at a time to our room.

You loom behind me in the mirror
as I brush my teeth with two fingers.
(Ugh! Toothpaste after too much wine!)
One glance assembles your dark eyes, my blond hair.

You slough off your wrinkly green and aubergine dress,
the sequins slinking over your slim waist,
and even in this unfamiliar place
there's a fine-grained sense of togetherness.

I turn out the light and darkness coagulates
in a delirium of tenderness...
There's a sound like sinuses clicking, then the pungencies
of moistened dust and freshened mould – a hiss –

it's rain, throwing itself sideways
through the open window, touching our cheeks,
eyelids, lips, slapping the roof-tiles with all
the relief of coughing in the intervals of a symphony,

and with no lights other than strafing headlights,
the air tense with electrocuted insects,
I sense your presence like a snake that cannot hear
but feels sound as a subtle and luxurious

massage along the whole length of its body.

A Game of Chess

A white, cordless telephone on the lawn and
your breasts gibbous under a cricket jumper

are the still points of the afternoon,
supporting a mower's ebb and crescence,

laundry stiffening in the breeze, moving this way,
that way, like the gills of a healthy fish.

The grass has that manufactured look like
the felt at the bottom of our chess pieces.

You sit opposite me with patrician disdain.
Your Queen bursts through my defences

like the Lord's streaker, before being escorted away.
First the Bishop's mincing *politesse*,

then the Knight, awkwardly received, lead a recovery
but it is the lumpen button, substituting for a lost pawn,

that proves your undoing, wriggling
with spermy improbability to the end of the board.

Blue Territory

Railway wires thread stitch after stitch
through the wet darkness
of towns between Manchester and London.
Lights shake tinily in the wind.

I miss you and am bored by my book
of Italian short stories,
dry-throated and doped by the train's radiators,

then, suddenly, there it is –
a huge and luminous swimming pool brilliant under glass –
like a blue grotto
under a vaulted roof

setting off submarine glints,
as if an eye had opened gorgeously over the landscape,
or a sun had burst
to release a web of hot young stars...

The vision leaks into the night and subsides.
The noise of the train re-establishes itself quickly,
and we are rushed through the sinuous glooms.
At least I feel as if I'm facing the right way.

Approaching Euston, I consult a plan of the Tube.
If only our future could be mapped with that simplicity.
The blue line of the river runs across the city
like a premonitory vein across my hand.

Colloquies

1

I'm calling you, hunched under
the lurid plastic embrasure

of an airport payphone, full of anxious eagernesses
and frightened politenesses,

my heart making a fist.
Outside, the jets bank under cloud massifs

like pointy-brassièred Valkyries.
'If I had to spend a month with you, it would be February!'

Your voice would melt all the 64,000
butter-pats delivered weekly to Heathrow.

The departure times flutter their story-
boards as the pips go,

your words carrying in the wind
beyond the range of ordinary hearing.

With the ears of the passengers blocked-up,
I strap myself into the seat.

2

A coughsweet clicks against my teeth on the phone.
In my pocket: a taupy *Waterstones* bag,
four passport photographs, an I (heart) Dublin badge
and a Donor Card: a whole history

without footnotes. They deserve a collective noun.
I carry them around with me always. They
console me even on the wettest days.
They will command a fetishistic attention at my death.

3

It is Spring, and you are highly strung.
It has been six weeks since we have seen each other.
The sudden rise in temperature
has touched off alarms all over the city.

Coming home, the light-sensor clicks on/off in the dark,
triggering the flowers' innermost parts
into imitation Georgia O'Keeffes.
Words run dry between us.

Insects register the rise in our blood.
You play the martyr like the Mata Hari,
blowing kisses to the firing squad.
I outrage you with my sulking stubbornness.

Your eyes, lit from inside, move through their three colours;
your incandescent temper –
ruthless, Irish, hyperbolic,
flares like a forest fire over my head.

4

As I whittle a pencil,
the paint flakes like glitter
and pollinates my finger.
A helix of shavings unravels,

peeling off like eyelashes.
Sometimes, an over-attenuated lead
can shrug off its husk of wood.
This one by the phone has recorded many messages,

scrawled numbers and addresses in
a black leather book, torn
with age. I sharpen it, fastidious as an assassin,

and wait for your return;
my open penknife, like a cuckolded latin,
making the sign of the horn.

Sunspots

Sea and sky enjoy a long courtship.
A wince of light like silver foil
trapped between the teeth,

the ferry shooting bolts of foam.
One more shot to finish the film.
You stand at the ferry's stern rail,

your head tilted to one side,
an impish smile recovering the original
urgency of our love,

your eyes absorbing melancholy
the way
the sun absorbs its black bits.

The camera rewinds
with a protracted *râle*,
back-pedalling through

the voluptuous nostalgia
of this last month together,
stretching a thin membrane between

Manchester and Dublin,
between one who believes in
original sin

and has seen the light, and
one who watches the florid
pattern of the wake unwind –

the water tan
as shoe-wax, the sun,
like a penny, teasing at its lid.

Moonshots

Boxed in a room over the door of which is written
In Case of Fire Access to the Roof Through This Room,

I lie, fully clothed, on the covers of my bed
watching the lamp shed

its flaky gold halo.
Objects conjugate on the table,

their shadows wrongly placed –
the moon blazing in at the window.

*

The astronaut takes the elevator
up the gantry,
a piece of siege machinery
next to the rocket's white shaft.

He can still taste his breakfast.
He carries a survival kit in
a canvas bag, comprising:

an inflatable life-raft
shark repellant
a desalinisation rig
2 .45 calibre pistols
a magnetic compass
5 gallons of water
food concentrate
a solar-powered receiver/transmitter
signal lights
a knife
50ft of nylon rope

His family watch the launch on television.
Outside, querulous pressmen trample the lawn,
flashbulbs creating a storm
like sheet-lightning against the windows.

The family are photographed from flattering angles,
their smiles sunny-side up.

*

There is little or no mention of the Moon in the Bible
but this makes me like this talismanic
little rock even more. Prepared to take the long view, I pick
up my satellite decoder and flick channels.

*

Hands shield eyes in the gallery
at Cape Kennedy
as the lean torso of Apollo
is launched on a column of fire.

Nazi rocket scientists arraigned after the war
watch their baby burn
through the atmosphere
to the strains of *Also Sprach Zarathustra*.

*

'A voice interrupts the popular
orchestras, so seductive it borders on horror.
We huddle together
listening to the radio
like children wanting the same story read every night.
The window's double cameo
of landscape and faces equates man with nature better
than any nineteenth century novel.

They are coming – that much seems confirmed.
Outside, leaves fall, doomy, calendrical.
Though we have sugar and tea still
to last us a week, I prefer to take my chances.
I shoot my wife and kids, pour a drum of kerosene,
throw in a match and run for it.'

*

Three astronauts tumble *in utero*
around the gravity-free cockpit,
turning an excess of speed into repose –
the rhythms of man's last climacteric.

                    *

Scene:
          the powdery lunar surface,
the plantedness of
                    the Stars and Stripes.
Two astronauts
                    clumsily sublime
                              in slo-mo,
anonymous
               in outsize suits.
The sun appears
                    like a frizzed lace
teased
          through an eyelet,
throwing the moon's
                    curvature
                              into relief.
The light expands,
                    a shadow affirms itself,
a warmth radiates
                    outward,
disclosing our blue,
                    maculated planet,
its weather systems
                    streaked like the palette
of an Action Painting.
                    The moment
plays itself out
                    epically
on the astronauts'
                    dark visors.
Interface of moon
               and sun.

                    *

Companionable moon
'like a mirror when a lamp
in the next room moves.'

Jittery stars like
veins of space in a page of type
held up to natural light.

My hand moves
from the margin's crisp white space
to where darkness is typical,

mass critical,
and time turns itself inside
out.

*

In the 1962 fight between Richard Nixon and Pat Brown for the Governorship of California, the Nixon campaign issued anonymous leaflets with a photograph doctored to show Brown bowing to Khrushchev. The Democratic riposte was to make public a title deed signed by Nixon in which he promised not to sell his Washington house to a black or Jew. Nixon decided not to respond to this charge according to senior aide John Ehrlichman 'upon the premise that deep in their hearts most of the people who would vote for him approved of such covenants'.

Seven years later, as President of the United States, his voice carrying forever on loquacious air-waves, Nixon claimed the Moon on the behalf of all humankind.

*

so yuz
thought
yud git
ther
first didja
com-
rade?

*

My nail engages the pawl,
  my little finger trawls
in the slack on the cassette.
  I put on my earphones but forget
to switch off the speakers, so that
  the songs of Weill and Brecht
bloom from the stereo.

Curtain hooks, like a series of bass clefs,
  wait to be placed on the stave,
Beyond the uncurtained window,
  the blue changing glare of television sets.
The moon paints itself into a corner.
  A cloud puts the moon under its jumper
and runs with it.

                    *

The tension of re-entry
and the capsule
parachutes down with its caul
of silky filaments
into the Pacific.

The heroes return, stepping out,
wings dry, into the light.
They will meet the President,
though they won't bring home
venereal disease like Columbus.

They are accorded a tickertape welcome.
Fired by a new largeness of ambition,
they will become Senators,
alcoholics, religious zealots,
and bruise easily.

                    *

The moon is theatrical in its guises.
It is an improbable Forces' Sweetheart.
It is an exquisite cadaver in a boneyard.
It is a glabrous mannequin.

It is a rearview mirror for the sun.
It is white as an iceberg on the White Star Line.
It is thin and slippery on the ice.
It has long been subject to a hose-pipe ban.
It is blotchy as a tambourine skin.
It is unevenly inked as a rubber stamp.
It would make a first-rate open prison.
It is published in a new *Pléiade* edition.
It glints and turns like a coin twisting through water.
It enjoys the residual glamour of *film-noir*.
It is a Hollywood *mise-en-scène* projected at our backs.
It has the authenticity of a watermark.
It is a chip off the old block.
It is the nine o' clock watershed.
It is florid and approximate as an artist's impression of a man
    in the dock.
The sun smears the moon in honey, then licks it off.
It is stately as a swan or ship on a box of matches.
It has a low blink-rate.
It wrings its hands over bone-coloured rocks.
It is not 'collectible'.
It is true, the Vikings got there first.
It is green and Lorcaesque.
It is the ultimate sexual conquest.
It is a supernumerary pap.
It inspects its pate in the burnish of a hubcap.
It is prized for its broad handling of light.
It grows like something left on a petri dish overnight.
It is the nightglow on the ceiling during insomnia.
It describes the surface of things as though it were their souls.
It makes good advertising copy.
Like music, it has no morality.
It turns a blind eye to atrocities.
It rises over the city like the first note of *Rhapsody in Blue*.
It is an itsy-bitsy yellow thong.
It is a head suspended forever.
It was thrown by Salomé from a sheer promontory into the sea.
It renews itself like the golden bough.
In the Festival of the Alphabet, it ports the letter 'O'.
It makes a slightly overripe version of *Me and my Shadow*.
Its unbuttonedness to commercial exploitation has shocked observers.
It is first stop in humankind's cosmic diaspora.

Its Hiltons will afford a better view than the *Jules Verne* restaurant
      in the Eiffel Tower.
Its profile affects a toby-jug hauteur.
It drops its handkerchief upon the waters.
It is a design statement.
It dangles, unlike its photograph, without a frame.
It shimmies in a miasmal do-nothingness and is contained.

*

The moon rises like a wrecking-ball
over the Great Wall of China.

Nixon shakes Mao by the hand.
Rev. Sun Myung Moon solemnises thousands.

*

Light flares in the high-rise
like a match being struck inside a beehive.
The sky blackens to a muddy slurry,
a soluble darkness pearled at the rim.

Empty office-blocks and shops stay lit all night.
Televisions are left switched-on
in empty rooms as if another civilisation
were trying to communicate with our own.

We are still accelerating away from ourselves,
from that repertoire of affects and memories
we archly refer to as 'background noise',
towards an undecoded landscape.

Remember the blind man who, given sight,
died with disappointment at the imperfection of the world?
He should have been driving home with me tonight,
witnessing a marvellous flaky beauty,

the moon now to the left, now to the right of the car,
the leaves vivid under the streetlamps, the house
drowned in subaqueous shadows, headlights
chamfering the angles of kitchen and bedroom walls.

*

Lionised by the romantic armchair traveller
of the Twentieth Century –
the moon and its memorabilia
now on sale at Sotheby's.

*

I walk for more than an hour in the early
evening dusk. Warming
streetlamps echo the hurt colour of the sky.
A tram scatters its shower of sparks, brushing

the pavement with the velleity
of an angel's wing.
A bluish moon lifts its wing-cases over the city
where the lights send up an amber glow.

I remember lying on my back, throwing
stones at night into the dark
and never hearing them fall, believing
they had gone on to found cities or stars.

It is the same moon my father showed
me as a six year old in 1969,
waking me at three in the morning to
tell me there were men on that globe;

the same moon Dante felt his body
penetrate as diaphanous lunar matter,
'lucid, shining, thick, solid and clean,'
and the same stars burning like an Allegory

on a burnished ceiling above the world,
their melancholy reflected in everything –
the beautiful abstraction of prime numbers,
voting systems, the sumptuous nothing

of religion, politics and art.
On their kitchen table this evening,
my mother's wedding ring, the constellation
of tablets my father now takes for his heart.

Patrimony

Heat throws a wobbly over the barbecue.
Tenderised steaks blacken over the charcoal
along with drumsticks mummified in silver foil.

The family gets together after my father's recuperation.
He has seen the film of his operation
and relished the sawing of ribs, the teasing

of veins into arteries. *Hoc est corpus meum...*
Now, for our benefit, he stages a performance:
bluff, incorrigible, sloshing too much red wine

down his gullet after too much red meat.
He handles the skillet like Karajan,
adjusting chops like crotchets on the bars of the grill.

He is reanimated like Disney *redivivus*.
But behind all the bluster, his
breathing is a touch more stertorous,

his handshake a little less firm. Like an
instrument thrown out of tune by humidity
his voice has risen a semi-tone.

And, as if the threatened paralysing stroke had come,
I notice how one
side of his face, despite itself, wants to cry.

My Last Wife

I tamp a fluffy roller in a cleated tray
upon a newspaper
dated December 12th: a birthday
shared by Gustave Flaubert and Edvard Munch –

a shush; the bubbled wallpaper
coming unstuck,
suppurating like an arm held over
a boiling kettle...

You always identified with Emma Bovary.
I always thought you were a scream.
I blend the tell-tale flecks to burgundy.
Tenacious little stains.

Time to unsheet the furniture,
to restore your photograph
which still insists on its inviolable place
in my life.

I work the blade of a Stanley knife,
tuggingly, around the glass frame.
The exiguous margins of card slither
like rind to the floor.

A Night To Remember

Unscrewing the valves, he spits on them
to make them quick and lissome, then
screws them back in, placing the ends
of his fingers on the nacreous tops...

The band-leader in his black tuxedo
holds his trumpet level for a solo.
Pungent gouts of smoke thicken over
the low-ceilinged room, clouding the bar mirror,

and settle into a fuggy crust above the glass.
As he squeezes air through the mouthpiece, the brass
tubes warm to his breath, the air cools
against the metal, turning to spittle

which leaks at intervals from the slides.
His temples are taut as a bicycle saddle.
His pudgy Cupid face flushes darkly from the strain,
right down to his empurpled lugs.

A cold gleam plays on the chrome bell's long throat.
The notes rise in a hurry of escaping bubbles.
The slow kiss of the music burns a bevel in his lips.
The melody enlarges then fractures in a web of tiny cracks.

Ice. Stars. The silence under water.

Sea-Fret

4 times disappointed
in love
she walks her 4
commemorative Alsatians

through vitreous repetitions
of stormlight,
herons – white chevrons
over a littoral of shards

and the suspension bridge
on a plinth of mist
filling the vacuum
with its poise.

Waves climb the calendars
of rock.
Gulls hog the promontories.
The sea sloughs off its dead scales.

Humber. Dogger.
Fisher.
The rebarbative
German Bite.

Tip-Toeing Around the Ego

*(In this poem, the ghost of Vladimir Mayakovsky
appears, following his suicide, before his Russian-born
Parisian lover, Tatiana Yakevlova.)*

I pass in front of
                    the projector,
scattering shadows upon
                            the screen of your dreams.
From my red Elysium
                        among the seraphim of Lenin –
I can see the city shimmer
                            its tambourine of lights,
snow in the streets
                    pressed like cerebellum
and you
        burning through the stages of sleep,
my image
        flared on your retina...

That first night, I remember,
                            I struggled at the wrist;
the cuff's hole
                too small for the button.
In the background
                    a languid piano congratulated itself.
I was irked by the company:
                            the refined hypocrisy
of unctuous bureaucrats
                        gladhanding Party fats,
then the sudden intimacy
                        as I saw you.
We shared a stare across the room,
                                distance diminishing effrontery,
each look conveyed
                    like a tray
carried high through a churning
                                mass of dancers –
clarifying instants which
                        transformed the space between us.

I made a beeline for you
                    as you pouted non-committally
before a sumptuous
                    still-life;
your legs twisted elegantly
                    about one another,
your hands nestling
                    decorously
                    a half-full glass.

Our introduction was like
                    the meeting of continents,
the quiver along
                    a fault-line.
I followed you
                    with all the fascination
for sheer movement
                    that exercised early filmmakers.

Love came
                    like a renaissance of the taste-buds
                    on stopping smoking,
delicious minutes spent surrendering
                    avowals of devotion,
made secure in the weight of
                    each quick reassurance.

But absence bred indifference,
                    passion paled to routine
and you rejected my caresses,
                    trailing beaux
like a comet drags
                    its afterbirth.
You were better impressed by that
                    Parisian diplomat.
My Renault was only chauffeured
                    because I couldn't drive!
Unchecked by guilt,
                    you left me, numb
                    as after an amputation,
dissatisfied with
                    my mind's world,

plaiting the strands of poetry
                    and sadness.
You devoured me like a snake that
                    swallows another twice its size,
leaving me
            unique and friendless,
pilloried by the critics –
                    myopic censors
running the touchlines
                of culture...

So I gambled on a bullet
                    and won,
fleeing this life
                for a disinfected heaven;
the honeymoon of water
                    after the thaw.
No dust in this museum,
                    no corrupting bugs
or filaments of decay
                    to brush away.
Here
        a higher mechanics obtains,
the colours splendid
                    like the colours in a coma.
(Only once or twice
                    I upset the angels
with my
        revolutionary argot.)
Of course, I have to endure
                    the ribbing of Esenin
writing me ironic sonnets
                    but I,
                        my voice Krakatoan,
smash the islands
                of his lines.
Ha! Now I sound bitter
                    but my grudges have run their course.
It's all so much ash
                trodden into the carpet.

Tonight,
          Tatiana,
                    as the moon says grace over the plains
and the wind-obedient fields of wheat
                              move in unison
like a flock of birds
               achieving equity of a kind,
I am restful,
          content,
                    no ridge on the finger
from writing any
          score-settling autobiography.
I have taken my place
                    in the Milky Way,
tackling the galaxy
               from heaven's pedestal,
sipping afternoon tea
               with the sun,
no longer gulping
          with embarrassment.
I float lightly as balsa
               on your consciousness –
a violin
     in an abyss.
I melt
     into formlessness,
deepening into
          layers and folds –
like landing lights, maybe,
                    or vapour-trails
strung across the sunset,
               like rope-burns
as they darken
          and dissolve...

Now everything is arranged,
                    in context,
taken care of,
          resolved to
the last
     retracted
          claw.